I BECAME HER TOO

I BECAME HER TOO

A NOVEL

LATRICE GLEEN

authorHOUSE®

AuthorHouse™
1663 Liberty Drive
Bloomington, IN 47403
www.authorhouse.com
Phone: 1 (800) 839-8640

Model's information:
Cover Model: Tommi Cole
IG, FB Twitter and Linked In @Tommicole

Editor:
Deidre Brooks

Photo Credit: Photographer - D. Austin

Book Design: AugustPride

Published by AuthorHouse   10/02/2015

ISBN: 978-1-5049-4810-4 (sc)
ISBN: 978-1-5049-4809-8 (e)

Print information available on the last page.

This book is printed on acid-free paper.

I dedicate this book to the memory of
"Jerome Tyree Robinson"
My Security
I miss you buddy.

INTRODUCTION

We continue on Samantha's journey in "I Became Her Too".

Samantha, as we know, is very successful when it comes to handling her business. She has a beautiful family and a man who truly adores her. With all these great things going on in her life you would think she couldn't make any wrong decisions, right? Samantha almost lost it all with one bad decision that almost cost her everything.

Samantha's problem has always been "being too independent" she is usually giving orders, so it's hard for her to take orders. Samantha finds it hard to trust and give her heart away 100% to anyone except her daughter due to experiences with men in her past relationships, including Aniya's father. In "I Became Her" Samantha received papers stating that Aniya's father was going for full custody of their daughter after not being in her life for the first year. Samantha was upset about the entire situation.

Will Samantha lose this battle?
When it comes to love will she win or lose?
Will she marry Edward?
Can she learn to submit to him and only him or will she destroy her happiness because she can't resist the temptation of other men?

The person sometimes with what we see as "the perfect life" is not always happy inside because of fear of not deserving a good man. Samantha has her career on lock and her beauty is breath taking, she has the ability to turns heads as soon as she walks in a room. But something is missing from her life.

Let's continue on Samantha's journey and find out who did she become.

I Became Her Too

TABLE OF CONTENTS

"A child with a married man brought a custody battle"
"A women with trust issue's brought doubts"
"Sex brought pleasure"
"A good man brought love"
"Betrayal brought violence"
"Hurt and violence brought pain"
"Pain almost cost someone their life"

CHAPTER 1

NEW BEGINNINGS

Laying in the bed looking at the clock on the night stand, it read 8:17am. Samantha decided to get up early while the rest of the household was asleep. She knew Edward would be sleep for at least another hour. She looked at Edward while he was sleep and smiled, thinking to herself, "I'm finally happy". She then walked out of their room and into Aniya's room and watched as her baby slept peacefully. Next, she went to Jr.'s room which was across from Aniya's. She couldn't help but laugh as she looked at Jr. (while he was sleeping) with one leg on the bed and the other leg hanging off of the bed. Leaving the kid's rooms, she proceeded to walk down the hall and down the stairs to the kitchen so she could prepare breakfast. This was the first Saturday in a long time that she had time to actually cook a full breakfast. She pulled out the sausages, eggs, grits and bread and then went up to her bathroom to brush her teeth and wash her face. As she returned back into the kitchen she grabbed the frying pan and all the cooking utensils she needed to prepare the families breakfast. As she went to crack her first egg she heard a little voice coming down the stairs.

"Mommy," said Aniya.
"Yes, baby... you are up early...what's wrong?" asked Samantha
"I want to get in your bed," said Aniya.
Samantha replied, "Awww sweetie, you know you can't get in my bed especially when Edward is sleep because we don't want to wake

him up, go back to your room and try to lay back down while mommy finish cooking breakfast."

Aniya looked at Samantha with a sad face that only she could make.

"Come give Mommy a kiss and a hug baby girl," said Samantha.
Aniya smiled and walked to her Mom and gave her a big hug and kiss and said, "I love you."
Samantha replied: "I love you too, baby. But let's get you in that bathroom and freshen up that mouth...you know we have to have fresh breath because we are princesses."

Aniya laughed as her mom tickled her and they went upstairs together and Aniya went to brush her teeth and wash her face.

1 hour later - 9:38am.
Breakfast is served.

Everyone is sitting at the table and it's a must in their household that a prayer is said to bless the food prior to eating. Edward usually would say the blessing.
"God, thank you for all of your blessings. Thank you for our family and our new beginnings. Bless the food my lovely fiancé has prepared for us. Amen."

As they are eating Jr. burst out of nowhere and said,

"Samantha, you can cook, this is some good food!"
Samantha laughed and replied "So, are you saying that your Dad can't cook?"
"Yup. He can't," said Jr. as he looked at his Dad and laughed.
"Samantha," he continued, "is it ok if I call you Mom?"

Samantha was in shock and kind of caught off guard and didn't really know how to reply as she looked over at Edward. Edward gave her a nod implying it was ok.

"Well, how about you can maybe just call me *Mamantha* instead of Samantha," said Samantha.

Edward thought that was funny as he repeated her, "Ma Mantha. Can I call you that too?"

"No, crazy," said Samantha.

2pm.

"Baby, what do you have to do today?" asked Edward.

"Finish unpacking and try to get this house in some type of order. I have to contact the office in Atlanta and see what's up with the magazines for next month's edition."

"So are you going to look for an office here? I think it would be easier to bring everything and just work from here."

"I couldn't leave my staff without a job. It will work out. I'll just start a separate magazine in this area under my company and let my assistant and VP handle Atlanta but I would still have to travel between both offices."

"Okay. Well, I'm about to head to work. I'll be home about 11:30 tonight and don't throw my stuff out."

Samantha laughed, "What stuff? You mean your junk? This house needs some life. Especially the living room. I'll have it poppin' with color."

"Whatever you say. And, oh yeah, Jr. has to go to my Mom's at 6pm don't forget. Now, get over here so I can feel you up before I leave."

"Yes, sir!" said Samantha as Edward grabbed her butt and started rubbing it while holding her body close to him before forcing his tongue down her throat.

"Geesh, babe," she said as she pulled away. "Where you think I'm running off to?"

"Nowhere at all because I got all that, but I just wanted to remind you who was the man."

Samantha laughed, "Get your crazy butt out of here!"

"I love you *Mamantha,*" said Edward.

"I love you too, Poopsie," said Samantha.

Edward proceeded out the door for work.

"Black and blue," said Samantha to herself as she looked at the living room. "I have to add white in this room it's just too dark in here".

Samantha continued unpacking and rearranging. She went to two stores to get some vases, pictures and area rugs. The kids enjoyed getting out the house for a little while and she had to take Jr. to his grandmother's house anyway. For the rest of the day Samantha spent time getting the house in order. She was so exhausted after she cooked dinner and got Aniya ready for bed. She had plans on watching a movie but she fell asleep in the process only to be awakened by a kiss on her cheek by Edward who returned home about 11:45pm.

"Baby," said Edward as he kept kissing her on her cheek and neck.

Samantha would move but not acknowledge him or even realize he was kissing her.

"Samantha," said Edward.

She lifted her head and replied, "Yes?"

"Come on and get in the bed", said Edward.

"In a minute," said Samantha as she closed her eyes again.

Edward laughed. "Baby, I love what you did to the house but come on and get in the bed before I wet you all up."

"What?" replied Samantha.

"Yes. *Wet you up* and not from me making you wet but from me pouring water on you."

"You play too much. Okay. I'll get up."

Samantha grabbed the remote and turned the TV off as her and Edward walked through the kitchen and up the stairs to their bedroom. While in the bedroom Edward decided to shower and then attend to his baby. He rubbed her down from her head to her toes until she was knocked out sleep. Samantha jumped up out of her sleep about 2am and looked at Edward; she looked around the room and ran to Aniya's room to check on her. As she walked back to her room she began to cry. She tried to be quiet but Edward didn't miss a beat. As she climbed in the bed he felt her and he immediately sat up.

"What's wrong," asked Edward?
"I just had a nightmare," said Samantha.
"Do you need to tell me about it," he asked.
"No," said Samantha, "I'm ok. Just go back to sleep."

Samantha didn't get that much sleep that night because she kept trying to figure out what the dream could possibly mean. The next morning she made sure she wrote it down in her dairy.

Dear Diary,

I had a crazy dream last night. I think Aniya's Dad is out to get me. In the dream he came in the house and I'm not sure whose house it was but when he came in he made love to me in such a passionate way and told me he wanted us to be a family. In the dream I believed him and let him stay the night. The next morning I woke up and he was gone with my baby. I called his phone and the number was changed and on my way to his house I woke up. That dream was scary, no way could I tell Edward because he will get to thinking that I was thinking about Aniya's Dad because I dreamed about him.

Sunday Dinner is always at Edward's Mom's house. Samantha went and enjoyed dinner with the family but left early to get some office work done while the kids were with Edward. While working she decided to call her friend Nita.

"Hey Boo," answered Nita.

"Hey, girl. I miss you. I have no one to visit, go out with or act a damn fool with."

"I know I miss you too, you know I don't like Bitches. How is everything going?"

"It's going good. Actually, it's too good to be true. You have to come visit me and soon."

"I will. I promise. Knowing Edward, he will probably kick my crazy butt out his house, you know that's my boy but sometimes I think he forget that I'm the reason yall together."

"Aint nobody studding Edward. He be at work all day and half the night."

"Did you hear what happen with Reggie?"

"Naw. What now?" asked Samantha?

"I heard he got caught up in some trouble and he about to be doing a few months in jail."

"Wow," said Samantha. "It must be serious. I haven't heard from him. I'm sure he will be mad when he finds out I left town and didn't contact him."

"Girl please. Fuck him. He doesn't need any explanation."

"Nita, I know but we still had a good friendship. I'm so scared here. I really don't know how I'm going to do all this; the business, the kids and Edward. I need my time to myself and I barely get that, shit it's a struggle to go to the nail shop. I have to travel back and forth a lot too".

"I'll help you if I can. You tell me what you need me to do at the office. You know I'm clueless when it comes to that corporate stuff."

Samantha laughed, "Girl, you don't even like writing a letter. I need someone to oversee my publications prior to print, just in case I can't be there to approve and sign off on it and I can't afford to employee anyone else at this time. My staff doesn't believe in deadlines and I can't be there to stay on their asses. It's a major challenge and the VP travels more than me!"

"I can help you with staying on their asses," Nita laughed.

"Yeah, I bet. They will all be ready to quit!" Samantha laughed before continuing, "Have you seen Aniya's father around anywhere?"

"No I haven't. Have you talked to him?"

"No, I'll see him in court in about 28 days. I can't stand that bastard."

"I never thought I'd hear the day that you would have so much hate in your heart for him"

"Nita, I don't hate him because he gave me my little princess but I hate his actions when it concern's her, you know? This guy was gone for over a year and then you just come back around and think you taking my baby from me, he is crazy as hell."

"It will all work out for you, he aint going to win", replied Nita.

CHAPTER 2

SPITEFUL

1 year has passed and Samantha has been back and forth with the custody battle between her and Aniya's Dad. They had to do a DNA test to make sure he was the father because he was not listed on the birth certificate. Aniya's father lied so much in court saying he had been in Aniya's life and the times he wasn't it was because Samantha kept him away by changing her phone numbers and not contacting him. He told the court that she took his child away because she was mad at him. He wants a fair relationship with Aniya and believes he deserves it. In Samantha's defense she was able to use pages out of her dairy to prove his absence and the reasons why but when the judge asked Samantha, "Do you want Aniya's father in her life?" She answered, "Yes".

He also asked if she feared for her child's safety and she answered, "No" because she knew she would be well taken care of in his presence. The judge granted joint custody with rotating holidays and summers. For the school year when she starts school she is allowed to be with her mother. The judge stated it would go in effect in January and she will be with her Mom for this summer but Easter, Thanksgiving and Christmas she will be with her father.

Samantha was pissed in court but there was nothing she could do. After court Aniya's dad went to speak to Samantha and she gave him the meanest look, if looks could kill he would have dropped dead in that court building. Samantha continued to walk away not acknowledging him at all.

"Samantha!" he yelled "Can we talk?"

She continued walking until she made it outside to her rental car and she drove off and headed to the office to finish up the work for next month's magazine edition. She was so frustrated she had to call Edward to try and ease her mind.

"Hey Poopsie" she said.
"Hi Baby. How is it going?"
"It's going ok. Where is my baby girl?"
"She is taking her nap right now"
"Oh ok. Well....the judge gave him joint custody."
"Babe, did you think he wouldn't?"
"Oh God, I didn't want him to Edward."
"Sam, listen. He deserves to be in her life, too, baby."
"No the fuck he don't." said Samantha with base in her voice.
"Ok, Calm down. I'm on your side. We will talk about it when you get home. I don't want you more upset.
"Too late, Bye." As she hung up on Edward.

Edward called her right back

"WHAT", screamed Samantha.
"Samantha, I am Edward. I need you to realize who you just hung up on and check your tone. Why you mad at me?"
"Because you're a man."
"Oh really", as he laughed. "I'm not just a man but I'm *your man*. Now apologize to your man."
"I'm not laughing Edward, I'm mad. I'm sorry and I'm hanging up now. I'll talk to you later.
She hung up and Edward called her right back.
"You forgot to tell me something" said Edward
"I love you" said Samantha.
"Ok, I'll talk to you later Babe"

Samantha put all her frustration and energy into her work. She needed to have everything finished before going home the next day. Samantha's next focus besides the office was trying to find the time to make her wedding plans. Samantha finished her final edits for the next edition which was scheduled for January (which was only 6 weeks after their wedding date). They decided to do it in October on the 18th because they wanted to keep it small since everyone can't make it to Florida. Edward didn't want to do it in Atlanta so Samantha didn't care if she had a big wedding or not, she planned to do a summer reception the following year.

Samantha wrapped up at the office and said all her good byes to her staff before heading out to the airport.

While sitting at the airport waiting for her flight Samantha broke down. "Lord, why am I doing so much all at once. I can't do it all. It's happening too fast. I need help. When I was single I never had to worry about all of this but I'm thankful for a good man I just want to be in Atlanta. She quickly pulled herself together before people around her started looking at her. It was time to board the plane and as she went to turn her phone off she noticed six missed calls. Two calls were from Aniya's father and she skipped over his messages. One message was from an unknown caller. When she played the message, it was Reggie's voice. She didn't have time to finish listening to the message but was shocked to hear from him. Her flight was being called and she had to get on the plane immediately. It was something in her that said "call him back". It was something about him that she missed and before getting on that plane and turning that phone off she listened to the message one more time. "Hey Baby, this is Reggie, I hope you haven't forgot about an old friend. I thought I'd give you a call to see how you were doing and to see if you would like to go out for dinner one day. Call me back, 404-404-4040.

She turned the phone off and just sat on the plane thinking about Reggie and how he did her in the past and wondered if he was still with his girlfriend.

Samantha arrived back in Tampa and Edward picked her up from the airport. While in the car it was an awkward quiet. Samantha sparked up a conversation.

"Edward, Where are the kids?"

"They are with my mom for the night."

"Why", she asked. "I need to see my baby."

"I think we need a night to ourselves and since you hung up on me I haven't spoken to you besides you texting me to pick you up."

"Edward I just want to shower and go to sleep when we get to the house."

"Really? Well I just want my fiancé to act like she loves me and what you want tonight might not go your way."

"Whatever", replied Samantha.

They arrived home and while in the house Samantha began to prepare herself to get in the shower. Edward walked up to her and grabbed her face.

"Please let me go Edward," asked Samantha.

Edward replied, "Shut up Samantha. Okay? Just shut up. What the fuck is your problem?"

Samantha said, "Why is it a problem if I say I don't want to be bothered?"

"Because I don't give a fuck about you not wanting to be bothered. I'll just keep bothering you," replied Edward.

Samantha always knew Edward demanded attention and she usually would give in but she really wasn't in the mood.

"What, Edward, what do you want from me. What?!!!!"

"First off, who do you think you are talking too? Second, I need you to respect the fact that I'm a man and I'm your man. Your mouth is too smart"

Samantha pulled away and walked in the bathroom, locked the door and got in the shower. Edward got upset and waited until she came out the bathroom. As soon as she opened the door he grabbed her and pulled her to the bedroom.

"Samantha, you can fight me tonight or you can love me tonight. It's up to you but if you want to fight you won't win."

She ignored him

"Samantha, you better answer me."

"Edward, I'm not a child. You want to know what the problem is? Aniya's father is the problem. I want to see my daughter and she's not here because you want to fuck me. That's the problem. Me being away from my company is the damn problem. Me trying to prepare for a wedding is the problem and you staying on my fucking back is a problem too. There are you happy now? Damn!"

"Fuck Aniya's father, he don't control how you act in this house. The problem was you were sleeping with a married man. Own that shit and deal with it. Your business is doing well. You could move it here. I'm sorry you feel like I'm always on your back. Maybe I should have left your lonely, selfish, stuck up and independent ass in Atlanta. You know what? Fuck us and fuck the wedding. Cancel that shit"

Edward stormed out the house and drove off. Samantha was so into her own feelings she let what he said go in one ear and out the other one. She wrapped her hair up and went to bed unbothered. She wanted to get married but the stress of everything made her not care if it happened or not.

3:15 am
Edward gets in bed.

"Samantha wake yo ass up! (he pushed her on her shoulders) Samantha!"

"Oh my God. What? Ugh, you stink! You smell like alcohol. Go to sleep Edward."

13

"Baby, fuck me right now. I need to feel you". He then kissed her face.

"I'm tired Edward. Promise. In the morning."

"No, I want it *now*."

Samantha gave in because she knew he would keep asking until she did it. She made no sound and showed no interest as she got on top of him and started riding and grinding on him as if it was his last time he would get some for a while. Edward started talking while Samantha was on top of him.

"Yes Sam, Yes Baby, ride this dick, don't stop (he started grabbing her breast and butt very aggressive and then he put his hands around her neck) "Don't stop, baby don't stop."

Samantha noticed he was getting too rough.

"Ok, Baby... you hurting me."

"Shut up and take it." replied Edward

Samantha has never had a problem with him being rough but this was over the top. His hands seemed to keep tighting up around her neck.

"Edward I know I'm fuckin you good but, Baby, I need you to not grab my neck so hard, just ease up a little bit."

"Tell me you love me Sam, Say it...."

"I love you Edward, I love you baby, you know that."

Samantha continues to give it to him as she rides him. Edward couldn't say anything but, "Yes....ooohhh...yesssss...yesssss. I'm coming Sam...ohhhhh…"

Edward was done and released his hands from her neck and as soon as he did that Samantha smacked him in his face.

"What the fuck was that for? Damn..."
"I told your dumb ass you were hurting me."

Samantha actually got a kick out of seeing his face when she smacked him and she was hoping he didn't smack her back.

"I'm sorry Sam; damn. I can't believe you smacked me. You know you not no gangsta. I would never hurt you. I love you."

Samantha got up to wash up and get a glass of water, when she returned back to bed Edward was knocked out already snoring. She did her usual routine when he went to sleep after sex, she would go wet a wash cloth and wash his penis off. Samantha layed down and went to sleep.

Good Morning 9:17 am.

"Baby, what time do you have to get the kids," asked Samantha?
"Not until about 5, why?
"Just wondering."
"Edward do you remember last night. You were very drunk and aggressive. That shit scared me.
"Baby you know I don't drink that much. I don't even remember driving home. I think I had about 10 shots last night. You had me ready to break your face"

"If I ask you to leave me alone it's not being mean its just time I need to myself and that's all I needed for about an hour or two."
"Samantha, you aren't single anymore and sometimes you walk around here as if you are. I'm here to help you if you are upset or angry you can't push me away all the time."

Samantha started to cry and just laid her head on his chest and he held her. She is starting to feel overwhelmed with everything.

"Baby I love you and I don't want to see you hurt," said Edward. "Everything will work out. Everything is not always going to be perfect."

Samantha started mumbling. "I failed her, I failed my baby. She has to go away with her Dad and be away from us and it's not fair."

"Its ok, we will make it work out the best we can. We get her more than he does. He just has a few summers and holidays. I'm here to help you get through it. Aniya loves you but she needs a relationship with her father".

"I hate that bastard," said Samantha.

CHAPTER 3

I DO

October 18th
3:30pm

"I now pronounce you husband and wife. Mr. and Mrs. Jones. Mr. Jones, you may kiss your bride," the minister beamed at the happy couple.

Edward couldn't wait to kiss Samantha, as she walked down the aisle, he couldn't believe this lady was about to be his wife—and now she was. He was amazed when he saw her. She was just as beautiful today as she was when he first met her. Her beautiful white dress fit her so well and showed her shape perfectly. The dress was off her shoulders with crystals outlining the top. She didn't need much jewelry. She had on pearl earrings and a nice diamond necklace with a pearl drop in the middle. Her make-up was flawless and all Edward could think of was kissing her beautiful glossed up lips.

Edward went in for the kiss and it was a long kiss. Samantha had to pull away because she didn't want her guest to think they were about to get busy on the altar, although that kiss was the most passionate kiss she had in a while. They proceeded down the aisle and greeted their guest in the hallway until it was time for the reception. Everyone was seated at the tables waiting for what was next.

"I would like to say congratulations to my best friend and her husband," Nita began. "I never thought Samantha would go through with this. She was so use to being free prior to meeting Edward, but Edward hurried up and put that thang in check." This brought an outburst of laughter from the wedding guests. Pausing to wait for everyone to quiet down, she then continued, "Edward you are a great person. She deserves you and you both deserve each other. I remember the first day you two met. I guess you guys can thank me for kind of hooking you up. Congratulations and I wish you the best because if not y'all know I'm locked and loaded. I'll go to war to keep you two together forever. Cheers!—Oh wait. The kids want to say something." said Nita.

"My mommy and Edward are cute and they love us," said Aniya said shyly.

"Samantha, thank you for being my mom. I'm happy you and my Dad are together. I have a real family now," said Junior said warmly.

Samantha was trying to hold back her tears so she would not mess up her makeup. She definitely didn't want raccoon eyes from her black eye liner. She stood up at the table to say a few words.

"Thank you all for sharing this special day with us," she said pausing to look into the faces of all the guests. "It has been a long journey and I guess I'll take the blame for it taking so long. One time Edward called me selfish. It was a reality check. I had to learn that life is not just about me and Aniya—although that's how it had always been—but it is about family. I love my family and my mom has been amazing. Although she doesn't know," she paused, again, as she looked directly at her mother, "but I appreciate you mom. My husband, Mr. Edward—you are everything to me and I love you. I'm not sharing you ever."

Edward stood up and kissed Samantha.

"Ok, I guess it's time for the man to say a few words but I really don't have much to say except to thank God for answering my prayers. Samantha was one tough cookie but I have her. I promise to love this girl and Aniya till my death," and true to his nature, Edward kept it short but he didn't lack sincerity.

"Ok, that's it. Where is the damn tissue and a fan? These eyes can't take it," said Samantha.

They had a nice reception and danced the night away. The reception had everyone smiling, drinking, dancing and enjoying each other. Edward's Mom was happy for them. While on the dance floor, Samantha's Mom pulled her aside.

"Hey, my baby girl. You are married now and I'm happy for you. I miss you and Aniya so much in Atlanta," her mother said squeezing her hand. "You know, I never really thought you'd get married but you did. I know you love me. We need to communicate better. You have a busy schedule and now you're so far away. You are out of my reach."

Samantha's mother smiled, though kind of sadly.

"Mom. I'm only a call away. You know I travel back and forth to Atlanta for work. I promise to do better with keeping in contact with you and letting Aniya come and spend some time with you." Samantha pulls her mother into a tight hug. "It's ok Mom. I love you."

Samantha, Edward and the kids went on a trip to Hawaii for a family honeymoon. They decided to take the kids with them because from that point on they would all be together. They were gone away for a week.

CHAPTER 4

BUSINESS AS USUAL

December

This is the year end of Samantha's magazine. The final issue to be printed for the year and since returning from the honeymoon, she had been working nonstop to make sure everything was done perfect and complete. This was also the month she had to send Aniya to stay with her Dad for the holiday. Her mind has been all over the place. She decided when she took Aniya to Atlanta she would stay a day or two and check on everything at the office. She wanted to see how the sales were going for the December's issue.

While cleaning around the house, the phone rings.

"Hello", answered Samantha.
"Hey Boo", replied Nita.
"Hi, my best friend. What's up girl?"
"I'm just sitting here reading your magazine and I have to say you're one bad bitch," Nita says the last part with nothing but respect and praise.
"Why you say that, crazy?"
"The *Don't Settle* article. Girl, you almost got me up dancing while ready to read this and punch myself at the same time!"
"You're a nut but if you like it I can only imagine what others are saying."

"Trust me. *They are loving it*. You nailed it. This is the best article yet. You should write columns more often in your magazine. You ended the year with a bang. Fireworks honey," Nita's thoughts came running so fast her energy was contagious.

"Awww, thank you! I'm excited. I'll be home in a week to bring Aniya. When I get there we need to go out because I need a break and I haven't had fun since the wedding. It's been husband, kids, work and no play."

"Oh yes. You know we are turning up as soon as you get here. I will see you in a week." Nita was already thinking about what to wear.

"Ok, keep promoting the magazine to all your ratchet friends. They need a copy too."

They both died laughing on the phone.

Christmas came two weeks earlier for the family. Aniya would miss out on Christmas day this year because she has to go away with her father. Samantha and Edward decided to have a pre-Christmas dinner and open a few gifts before she had to go away.

December 10th - The night before takeoff.

Edwards's mom joined them for dinner. The menu consisted of: ham, green beans, mac-n-cheese, rice, cornbread, peach cobbler and Ice Cream.

"God, we thank you for bringing us together to share this special dinner and we bless the food and bless the hands that prepared it, which would be my beautiful wife. Amen," Edward winked at Samantha who blushed.

"Boy you are a mess," Edwards mom said playfully in response.

"Mommy, I don't want to go with my dad," Aniya reaching for one of the homemade rolls.

"Sweetie, I know and believe me I don't want you to leave me but your dad loves you very much and you will have fun with him," Samantha encouraged her.

"It's okay," Junior interjected, "you will have gifts to open at his house, too."

Aniya smiled as her new brother looked at her.

"Baby Niy, you are not staying there forever. We will be waiting for you when you get back," said Edward.

To keep things in the spirit of celebration, Samantha decided to change the subject. "I have some good news about the magazine. It's doing really great and my assistant said they can't keep it on the shelves. They keep selling out."

"That's good," replied Edwards Mom. "You need to get them in some stores here."

"I've been thinking the same thing, that's on the agenda for next year."

"Hot damn! My baby is a star *and* she can cook. I hit the jackpot with you Samantha," Edward teased—although appreciatively.

"You better know it baby, I can't deal with you," she chuckled.

The family exchanged gifts after they finished their dinner. Samantha packed her and Aniya's bags before putting her to bed. Junior was still up. At the age of thirteen, it was hard to tell him to go to bed.

11:10pm Samantha and Edward lay on the couch watching a movie.

"So, what are we supposed to do when you leave?" asked Edward.

"Well, I'll only be gone for two days. You and Junior can do father and son things," Samantha suggested.

"I'm proud of you with this joint custody situation."

"Thanks, but you know I still hate it."

Edward chuckling, "I know you do!" Taking his hands he started rubbing Samantha on the back of her neck. He raised her long black hair, moving it to one side; he started kissing her on the back of her neck and then kissed her on the cheek.

"Edward, is this your way of telling me you want me?" she breathed.

"I always want you. Our schedules are always so busy. We never get time to just love on each other," he paused between each sentence to kiss her.

"I know. Seven years ago we couldn't get away from each other. I never imagined we would even be together." Samantha stepped away gently and turned toward him. "By the way, how are your kids doing? Have you spoken to them?"

"Sam. I'm talking about us loving on each other and you bring up my kids. You just made my dick go down," Edward said looking at her sideways.

"I'm sorry, Poopsie," Sam said laughing a little.

"Damn babe," he paused and shrugged his shoulders, "They are good, their mom is still crazy and bitter. She hates me right now, but Junior makes sure he talks to them every week. I can't just call her to talk to my kids without hearing her mouth about me being married and all this other crap." Samantha could see that he was deeply bothered by the state of his relationship with his child's mother.

"I can only imagine," Samantha said before she continued brightly, "Hopefully one day she will let them come visit us."

"They old enough to come here without her permission. You know, my daughter is ready but her sister really don't care. I mean I raised them together but she has her own dad who ain't around that much." As he said this, Samantha felt her husband's shoulders slump. "Hey," she offered, "you should see if your daughter could come. That would probably make Junior happy. I'm sure he misses his big sister."

"Her ass probably grown just like her mom," he said this with a look of disdain. "I'll think about it. One smart word out her mouth to me would just make me send her right back."

"I wish her mom wasn't so bitter so the kids could just be ok without the drama."

"Ok, Sam," Edward cut her short, "next subject."

Samantha laughed, "I know she want all this good wood you be dishing out but its mine now."

"Your husband is ready to put this good wood inside of his wife because his wife is leaving him for two days"

"I promise that I won't put up a fight tonight."

(They immediately started touching, kissing, and breathing heavy.)

Samantha's phone started ringing.

"You better not answer that", said Edward.

"You know I have to answer it, it could be important," Samantha said untangling herself.

"If someone is calling this late, it better be an emergency," he snorted.

Samantha answered the phone without even looking at the number.

"Hello", answered Samantha.

"Hey, Baby," the caller said in a deep voice. Samantha looked Puzzled because she didn't recognize the voice.

"Excuse me. Hello?" She asked this time.

Edward is staring at Samantha looking just as puzzled as she was.

"Samantha. It's nice to hear your voice," the voice continued.

"Who is this?"

"Who is it Sam?" asked Edward.

Samantha shrugs her shoulders saying as if to say she didn't know who it was.

"I'm not sure who this is but it's late and I have to hang up now."

"No. Don't. Hey. It's Reggie," and suddenly the light bulb came on for Samantha.

She laughs it off so Edward doesn't suspect it's another guy on the phone.

"You crazy. Do you know what time it is? Me and Ed just sitting up watching TV."

"Who is Ed? Do you know what Reggie you talking to?"

"Yes, we can talk about that tomorrow when I get to the office. Don't try to stress me before I get there. Get some rest. We will talk tomorrow," and as abruptly as the phone call came into her evening, she dismissed it. Hangs up the phone really fast and turns it off.

"Sam, what was that all about?" asked Edward.

"That was Tom. He wanted to go over the numbers with the magazines. You know he be on it."

"He has to remember you're married and—" but before he could say anymore...

"Edward." Samantha interrupted, "Business is business and with me its 24 hours."

"That is going to change soon. But now back to this wood talk," Edward said teasingly.

Samantha couldn't believe that call she received was Reggie, she was nervous sitting in front of Edward. She never returned his first call and she had to do what she needed to do at that moment being caught off guard with her husband looking right at her. Edward called her attention back in exasperation.

"Samantha, can we please get back to us? I know you are thinking about work now, but I'm thinking about the kitchen counter, the shower, on the floor or wherever you want me."

"The shower sounds good to me. You better make sure Junior is sleep."

"You know that boy not sleep but he not coming out that room or off that game. Go get it started and I'll follow."

Samantha went upstairs to their room, lit a few candles, put on some music and she got undressed. She stood right in front of the bathroom mirror looking at her own body. She starts talking to her body. "You have some perky breast, girl. They be loving these breasts, your little waist and that round booty."

Edward entered the bathroom.

"Did you lock our bedroom door?" asked Samantha.

"Yes, Sam."

They both stepped into the shower. He stood in the shower examining his wife's body. He looked at those same perky breast and nipples as the water ran down her body. To him she had the perfect body with a nice shape. He started rubbing on her breast and sucking her nipples. He loved everything about her.

"Wait Babe, step out the shower." said Edward.

"Huh? For what?"

"Just do it."

Samantha stepped out the shower and he sat her on the bathroom sink counter after pushing all her smell goods to the side. He opened her legs and started to rub her clitoris with one finger and then he proceeded to kneel down and he took his tongue and started licking her down there while still playing with her with his finger.

"You taste so good baby"

Samantha couldn't say anything; she was trying to keep it all in. All she could do was moan and grab his head and squeeze his shoulders. Not two minutes later she started talking.

"Ooooh   Edward,   baaaabyyyyy...   Damn.... AHHHHHHHHHHHHHHH!"

She screamed so loud that Edward was not only grinning from ear to ear, but laughed.

"Why you so loud, you trying to wake up Aniya and what about Junior hearing us?"
"You should stop then," she matched his laughter. "You know I can't take it, I be trying to hold it all in."

They got back in the shower and Samantha took control of him. She grabbed his penis and began to stroke it up and down, she then started giving him head. Edward loved the way she made him feel when her mouth was wrapped around his penis. While licking, sucking and stroking Edward started moaning and grabbing Samantha by her hair. That just turned her on more and she wouldn't stop. She wanted to make him cum but Edward stopped her. Edward placed her up against the wall in the shower and let's just say he put his wood in his wife that night. Samantha couldn't hold it in. He covered her mouth and pumped harder and harder until he felt her tense up and start shaking. He knew she was good by then, so then he pumped more pumps and kissed her on her neck and started french kissing her until he finally came. They both were in the shower tired and ready to pass out after that. They showered and proceeded to get ready for bed.

"Edward, I love you. You always know how to keep me satisfied," she cooed.

"That's what I'm supposed to do. You are leaving me so I had to go in for the kill."

"She dead!" Samantha laughed.

"I love you Sam. Good night," and he kissed her on her forehead.

Atlanta - At the Office
3:56pm

Samantha arrived in Atlanta a little after noon. Aniya's father met her at the office to pick up his child. Samantha did her usual work, checking emails, reports, making calls, checking sales and meeting with her staff. She had one email from a friend Tee that she hadn't spoke to in a while. Actually she was pregnant with Aniya the last time they communicated. She had included her number in the email so Samantha decided to give her a call.

"Hello," answered Tee.

"Hi, Tee. It's Samantha."

"Hi, Samantha. I'm happy you called me," Tee says between a few coughs. "It's good to hear from you."

"Are you ok? You sound sick," Samantha asks with much concern.

"Yes, I'm ok, I'm ok," and Samantha can picture her throwing her hand as if to wave her off. "How are you? Lord knows I miss you girl. It's been so long, I think it was your baby shower."

"It sure was. Aniya is four years old now. I'm married and I've moved to Tampa."

"Did you marry her father? I know I've missed so much," Tee says with more than a little regret that she hasn't kept up with Samantha. That she let so much time pass.

"No way," Samantha exclaimed. "Oh God, no! He is still married to his wife." Pausing, she continued, "You know you shut me out. We never agreed on that situation."

"I know. I'm sorry. I've been dealing with life and so much more. I had to get in contact with you."

"So how are you? What's new and how did you find me?" Samantha then added with more than a little suspicion, "Maybe I should say *why are you looking for me?*"

"Can I just miss a friend? I actually have the December issue of your magazine. The cover is nice! I saw it at the newsstand and said, 'Wait. That's my girl on the cover.' I know you like to highlight others and this was different. Completely."

"Yeah. I just wanted to try something different to close the year out. No more cover pages for me though. If I still lived in Atlanta I would have never put my face on the cover."

"Do you remember that letter I wrote you about Charles?" Tee abruptly changed the subject.

"Of course I remember reading it. Just don't ask me to tell you what it said because I don't remember that," Samantha joked…a little.

"I told you to never give up on love," her friend responded kindly.

"Yes, you sure did." Samantha recalled thoughtfully.

"It looks like you didn't give up. I always thought you deserved better and I just wanted the best for you. What is your schedule like? When can we hook up?"

"Actually I'm in Atlanta now and I'll be here until tomorrow and if you want to hook up tonight. Nita and I will be going out this evening."

"Nita? Now wait… That's your crazy friend. Is she still crazy?"

"Yes. That's my best friend and she will always be crazy. But, hey, I love her. If you're not doing anything meet us at The Club downtown about 9pm."

"Only for you because I want to see you. I'll get some rest before I come out because I can't hang anymore," and it was true, but Tee's voice had a tinge of laughter.

"Ok," Samantha said, "See you soon."

JCLUB 9:45pm

The ladies were enjoying their night. Samantha was about 4 shots down and was all over the dance floor. She hadn't been out in so long that she almost forgot what it felt like to dance and dancing was her favorite thing to do. "Aint no feeling like being free," she is singing and dancing. Nita and Tee are right by her side breaking it down on the dance floor.

"You better sit your free ass down before Edward roll up in here." said Nita.
"Edward… *who?*" Samantha laughs
"Your husband, chile," Tee's southern accent on full tilt.
"Oh yeah, that guy. Yes, that's my husband," a slightly tipsy Samantha agreed.

The other ladies walk away to go sit down and leave Samantha on the floor when a dancing Samantha is approached by this guy dancing up against her. He smells good and all Samantha can see is his shoes, the bottom of his pants until she turns around and to her surprise it's Reggie. She stops dancing and looks at him in disbelief. She is impressed at what she sees and his cologne is really getting her hormones spinning.

CHAPTER 5

TEMPTATION

"Samantha, I knew it was you when I walked through the door. That hair, waist and those legs were a dead giveaway."

"Reggie, you know...........I really can't stand here and talk to your right now."

"You can't talk to me? Is your boyfriend in here?"

"No, but you look nice. I have to walk away from you."

"You leaving me out here on this dance floor, one dance...please?"

"I can't."

Samantha walked away feeling nervous but it was a different nervousness; she rushed to the bar with her friends.

"Omg, Its Reggie, I have to go."

"Why, we not leaving Samantha." replied Nita

"I'm tipsy, I can't be around him. I need my husband right now. Reggie smells so good y'all."

"Nita, do you think we should leave?" asked Tee

"Hell no, Samantha you better pull yourself together. You married. Reggie aint shit."

"That's my point, I'm married. I shouldn't feel tempted like this? I haven't been around any other men besides Edward and he smells so good."

"(laughing). You want to fuck him because he smells good." asked Nita

"(laughing) She probably do." said Tee

"No I don't. I'm just saying he smells good, I felt something and he danced up on me."

"Well I just scanned the bar and I think he is gone because I don't see him. No more drinks for you Samantha because you tripping." said Nita.

The ladies left the bar around 1:30 am. They had a good time together and it was much needed for Samantha. She forgot for a second she was a married 34 year old with a family at home. Nita drove Samantha back to her hotel and Tee drove herself home.

"Samantha, Tee looks small to me. What you think?" asked Nita.

"She did to me too but I didn't want to say anything. She doesn't look well."

"She looks stressed or something."

"Well, you know she be in her own world a lot, I'm not sure why it was so important to see me after she just disappeared on me. I need to go to bed."

"Go straight to sleep, what time is your flight?"

"About 5 o'clock."

"Ok, I'll call you're about 3pm."

They said their good nights as Nita watched Samantha walk into the main entrance of the hotel. Samantha stumbled going in the door and she even had a hard time getting in her room, she kept putting her hotel key card in the wrong way. Samantha is in her room and she has a few missed calls. She had a voice mail from Edward and one from Reggie.

She decided to call Edward.

"Hello?" Edward answered (half sleep).

"HI BABY."

"Sam, stop yelling. Are you drunk?"

"No, just tipsy."

"So, you went out and that's why you didn't answer your phone when I called you?"

"If I knew it was ringing I would have answered, I'm calling you now."

"(laughing) Go to sleep, its two in the morning."

"I want you right now."

"That's the alcohol talking. I'll see you tomorrow babe. Go to sleep."

"I can't, my head hurts."

"If you lay down you will feel better."

"Ok, Love you."

She hung up and laid down without even taking off her clothes. She really didn't want to lie down but she thought it was the best thing for her to do but even with her laying in the bed she couldn't go to sleep.

CHAPTER 6

THE MAGAZINE

The next morning she got herself up and out the hotel. She forgot she had a staff meeting at 9:30am, the night before was a great time but she only remembers bits and pieces of everything.

At the Office.

"Mrs. Jones you have nailed the December Issue of the magazine. We think you should write a column once a year." said her Assistant.

"Actually, this was a onetime deal. I'll continue to highlight others because I don't want the attention on me. It's so many other writers and designers that need to be highlighted. I received an email from a popular talk show host asking me to appear as a guest on the show. You all know I live a private life but with that cover photo it's not as private. You guys are the best staff and I appreciate you all. We are a team and Clyde is our security who keeps us all safe in this building. The business will always be in Atlanta and if I expand it won't be anytime soon. Lunch is on me today, it should be delivered soon. Until next time, let's continue to rock out this magazine in Atlanta. We ended the year the right way."

The staff was happy and they all clapped and hugged Samantha. Samantha had worked so hard building her magazine company and it all seemed to be coming together. She hoped to put someone major in the entertainment business on the cover in the near future. She was so overwhelmed with joy and the numbers in sales kept climbing. They couldn't print fast enough to keep the magazine in the stores in the Atlanta area.

"Ok, I'm heading back to my office to read OUR December Issue one more time." said Samantha.

CHAPTER 7

DON'T SETTLE

The Magazine
Atlanta
December Issue

I dedicate this column to my Love Jones.

I've always played the victim in relationships because I didn't know how to handle being hurt; used or abused but when he came into my life I became just like the ones who hurt me towards him. I was scared to let go fully and love again with the fear of being hurt. I had to learn how to love myself so I could love someone else better. He always was there no matter what I did and he showed me true love and the value of it. He has remained that same love from day one. I hope you enjoy this issue and happy new years to all my readers.

Don't Settle!!!!
"Easier said than done"

This edition is for my ladies. As women, we often blame the men who we allow in our lives for our hang-ups and problems but we are responsible for who we let in but most importantly who we let stay. We have to take the blame for compromising our worth. Often times as ladies we put ourselves in situations that we know are not good for us.

We do them for a lot of different reasons. Some may do it for the love of money, for comfort, for sex, just to say you are in a relationship or just because we as women don't want to be alone. I am a woman and I have been here plenty of times and I often find myself drifting back and revisiting some of these places in my mind. How or when will we stop this???

Let's Talk

1.) No Good For Me
2.) The Sex Is Great!!!
3.) I Don't Want To Be Alone
4.) He Does Love Me

1.) No Good For Me

Do you often find yourself saying those two words: NO GOOD?
You knew he was "no good" before you starting dating him.

> *Did you think he would be good for you when he had a girlfriend when you all first meet?*
> *Did you think he would be good for you when you know damn well he has kids that he does not take care of?*
> *Did you think he would be good for you when he does not have a job?*
> *Did you think he would be good for you when his last girlfriend use to get beat by him?*
> *Did you think he would be good for you when your brother told you "be careful"?*

Ladies, we have all been in these situations before, but some of us like the challenge, meaning we think we are "superior" to the other females he has been with prior to us. We often say *he won't do that with me* as if we have gold between our legs or as if we are the best he's ever had. Our value goes down when we mess with someone who has question marks by their name. A man will only do what we allow him to do. Kudos to you men because a lot of times, it's so easy for y'all to slide right in and slide right out whenever you want to and we as women be the damn fools crying over y'all and begging y'all to come back when we know damn well that you are "no good" for us.

Scenario 1: He has a girlfriend but he flirts with you and you like the attention. I mean really, who doesn't like attention?

You and this particular guy are really cool and he starts making passes at you. Touching your butt, giving you the eye and being extra nice to you and saying yes to anything you ask. He is a really great friend and he is someone you can talk to about anything. You don't know his girlfriend but you know he has one, you also know he has other female "friends" but you don't care because y'all are just cool. One day you two eventually take being friends to the next level and you end up sleeping with each other.

STOP!!!!

Ladies, as females we be trying to keep our emotions out of the equation and for the most part we can do it at first. However, the more you continue to hang or have sex with your "friend" the emotions will start to show!!!

CONTINUE…..

Now that you and this friend have taken it to a completely different level, you tell yourself I *got this*. You and he continue to be friends and hang out occasionally. You then start seeing his girlfriend come around and you still remain cool with the situation.

If you have guy problems you talk to him about it and he gives you some advice. He tells you that you deserve better and starts asking you questions as to why are you dealing with certain situations with guys. Now as women, you start questioning yourself and you start looking at your friend as someone who really cares about you and start to wonder if he could be the one.

We all have been here, so don't act like you haven't. You start saying *he is fun, cool, makes me smile, cares about me and we have a good time together.* This is where we as females mess up the game. Men can care for us and have all the characteristics mentioned above but it does not mean they want to be in a relationship with us. They want to keep it the way it is with no strings attached—which means just friends who occasionally have sex with each other. Sometimes men also forget that it's just a friendship and they start wanting things from us. They start wanting us to cook for them and we do it. Some men ask us to do laundry and we do it. It starts to seem like a relationship-you are doing everything that people in relationships do. But did you forget, he still has a girlfriend and now his girlfriend may start questioning you and her man's "friendship"?

Ladies, we know how trifling females can be and the word *friend* means nothing these days. I'll tell you all a little secret "I, too, was trifling." We often cover up for our bullshit and the man's bullshit. Some ladies won't though. If your "friends" girlfriend came to you and said "Are you messing with my Man?" what would you say???

The girl who cares nothing about the man or the girlfriend may say *"Check ya man"* or she may say *"Yes, if you were doing what you suppose to do, I wouldn't have too."*

The girl who cares about the man will say, *"No, we are just friends".* Now, sometimes it may just be that "a friend" and other times it may be more than just a "friend". That's up to us to decide because the Man will never tell. When in a relationship you will know the difference.

Number 1: If you have friends that I don't know about then I may believe it's more than a friendship.

Number 2: If you have a friend that you have not introduced me to then that's another possibility that it's more than a friendship.

Number 3: If your call log and inbox is that "friend" all in your phone then we have a problem.

Number 4: If she likes every stat and picture you post on social network then you both are GUILTY! Social media tells it all. Lol.

<u>Scenario 2</u> - Did you think he would be good for you when you know damn well he has kids that he does not take care of?

Ladies, if you have dealt with this kind of man, you know you are wrong especially if you knew this prior to dealing with him. But you will be surprised how many ladies are in these kinds of situations.

She has a child that her man takes care of but he doesn't take care of his own kids. He is buying her child things and buying her things but has not seen or has done anything for his own child.

Me, as a female, I couldn't imagine being with someone like this. Some females are heartless and they think, that's his problem, not theirs because they are his kids. I understand sometimes the child's mother of the girls boyfriend may be ignorant (because they may not be together she won't let him see his child(ren)).

Do I rock with females like that? Hell naw! Still, there are a lot of those out there. In this situation, I'm talking about the men who just don't take care of their kids for whatever the reason is. Maybe they don't like the fact that the child's mother is with someone else or maybe they just don't like the child's mother at all. Whatever the case, the man is still obligated to take care of HIS kids "first" and not his girl's kids.

Ladies ask yourself this: if your man had three kids and the mother did nothing for those kids, what would you do?? Would you help take care of them or would you say *that's his problem*? No one will admit the truth. There are females out here who don't like kids or don't want deal with a man with kids.

<u>Scenario 3</u>- Did you think he would be good for you when he does not have a Job?

HERE WE GO!! Now this is often a situation that goes on a lot. He may have a job; in some cases it may not a legal job. A lot of women take care of their man. The women go to work and pay all the bills while the man stays home and does nothing but get waited on. Why? Some females just like having a man at home. Some females can't sleep alone so they will do whatever it takes to keep that man in the house with her. They start thinking like *Well, if he wasn't here, I'd be paying the same bills anyway.* So sad, but so true. Riddle me this, WHY do females give men all their tax refund money??? I have done a lot of crazy things but that is one thing I have never done. Some females buy their man a car, a new wardrobe or they may give them money to flip and when they flip it they keep it. Lol! There is no way in hell I would give a man my tax refund money for any reason. In most cases the following year that same man ain't with you and you never will see your money. Make that man get a job. Actually, you can't make him. If he has no drive or determination to want to work, then you deserve everything that comes with the territory of him not working. I'm being so serious, ladies…wake up!!

Have I ever dated a man without a job?? YES. Did I do things for him? YES. Let me tell y'all another embarrassing secret. I once dated a street pharmacist and let him hold work at my house. I said I would never do such a thing but when he asked I said YES. Did I charge him a *storage fee*?? NO!! Did he chop me out any of that money?? NO!! Was I stupid as hell?? YES!! Did I think about the possibility of getting caught up in some shit??? YES?? Did I make runs??? YES!!! I look back now and I say *"What the fuck was I thinking"?* I use to talk about girls who got involved in stuff like that. I only did it for about a month but that was the most stupid thing I could have ever done. You have to go through things to learn from it. And I learned that I would never do that shit again. And once again, I'm sure some of you have done his before but won't admit it. Don't look at me and say "Oh my God" she was so stupid because you never know what you will do unless you're in that situation. I can't even tell you why I did it. It wasn't because I was in love with him—because I wasn't. But I know one thing; after that I only dated men with jobs!!

Scenario 4: Did you think he would be good for you when his last girlfriend use to get beat by him?

Ladies, it's crazy to me that we still will get involved with someone when we know he is or was a women beater. Don't get me wrong, yes, men can change and just because they did it in the past, doesn't mean they will do it again but you have to keep your guards up. I had a situation where I did not know off hand prior to dealing with this one guy, but while being involved with him, I heard about something he had done to a girl and she ended up in the hospital. Now there is always two sides to every story, she got busted doing something and he beat her. That is still not an excuse, so don't think I'm saying she deserved anything because no matter what the situation a woman doesn't deserve to be beat by a man. I remember saying the famous phrase "*he won't do that to me*" and he never put his hands on me but if I would have done something to make him want too, would he?? I believe he may have. I'm not sure but I demand a certain amount of respect. Have I been called a bitch, a slut and all types of names? Yes!! But when it comes to being physically abused, I don't play them games. I played that game before and I made a promise to myself never to get involved in those types of situations again. My question is what makes a women think a man won't put his hands on them? Ladies, we provoke men a lot of times and we have to learn to keep our hands to ourselves as well. I know I have a smart mouth and I have said harsh things to men in a lot of different relationships. One thing I do know is I know who to say it to and who not to say it to. I use to say things because I knew some guys wouldn't put their hands on me. It reminds me of the movie (you guess which one) when she kept getting in his face and kept talking until he just snapped and smacked her. I remember a girl getting smacked in public and I was in shock, it made me look at that guy with no respect, regardless to what she did to provoke the situation that was embarrassing for her to have been hit like that in public in front of everybody. The sad part about it is she still wanted to deal with him, he publicly humiliated her. We as women go through a lot and put up with a lot but we control what we allow. A man will do whatever we allow him to do. It's like a dog, if the dog keeps shitting in the house and all you do is say "Ima beat your ass" and clean up the mess, the dog is going to keep on shitting in that same spot. Dogs are smart, they look at you and be like "*she aint gon do shit*". You are still going to walk that dog, you are still going to feed that dog as well as give the dog treats. Men are no different, they know what they can get away with and they still will get rewarded with their treats. I mean— why wouldn't they do it???

2.) The Sex is Great!!!

But the sex IS great!!!

Ladies, would you rather be with a man and have great sex but no job or a man with a job and have whack sex?? I have had both and even though some people say sex doesn't matter, it's a lie! If that was the case why have sex at all? Sex, love making, foreplay and affection does matter and it can either help or hurt a relationship. People have a million and one reasons to cheat and if they can get GREAT SEX from somewhere else, please trust and believe they will. A man can do everything right and be the best person in the world but if the sex is not right there will always be a problem.

Scenario: This guy is a liar, a cheater and everything else you may want to call him but he satisfies you in the bedroom, so you deal with him just for that sexual pleasure. You find yourself saying *"I don't care what he does as long as he put it down"* and it becomes a sexual relationship. A lot of people have "jump offs" just for that sexual satisfaction. They don't care about anything else and don't want a relationship but when it's time to make that booty call they are praying the other party answers the phone. I myself may have had what people call "jump offs" but then again I don't consider them that because anyone I have had any type of sexual relationships with, I have been in some kind of relationship with and it wasn't just a booty call. I liked to date, hang out and do relationship-type of things but I also like GREAT SEX. It's sad because I did have a situation where the guy's sex was bad but he was a very nice guy and wanted to do a lot of things with me and for me. I'm built different than a lot of females, anybody else would have got all that they could have out of him and just handled the bad sex but I couldn't do that. It has to be some kind of emotional, physical or sexual attraction and with him it just wasn't there.

3.) Dont Want To Be Alone

But I *don't* want to be alone.

Ladies, stop fronting. Y'all know y'all have said this so many times. We are so quick to say, "I don't mind being alone. I'm independent and I have a toy." Lmao!!! No one likes being alone, not even a dog likes being alone. We like to have the comfort of somebody. Being alone is not the end of the world. I had to learn how to adapt to being by myself. When you are by yourself, you like things a certain way. I like to come home and my house is the same way I left it when I left it.

Some people act like it's the end of the world to be alone. PLEASE don't get me wrong it's lonely at times, but it's so peaceful. If you want company invite someone over or have a ladies night or a get together. It's very weak (my opinion) of a woman to say she can't be alone. Especially if she has kids. Take that alone time to focus on you, your kids and your career. Find yourself and get to know you. It's so much better within your own space. Being alone is not a bad thing; it just may take some of you out of your comfort zone. TRUST me. You will be ok.

4.) He does Love Me

He *does* love me...*doesn't he?*

Do you know what love is? I mean really? I thought I did until I was in my late 20's. Its more to love than just saying you love somebody or them saying they love you. I can recall having conversations with my friends and they would say, "He don't love you, because if he did he wouldn't treat you the way he does." My reply would be, "He does love me" and a lot of times we as women are so defensive when it comes to our Boo, we will stop talking to our friends because we think they just don't understand. I would never tell any of my friends that they're man doesn't love them because that's not my place. Some people may not even know what love is. Your definition of love may be different from mine just based off of different situations.

Take this scenario: what if you are a child and your parents say "I love you" and the way they show they're love to you is through

45

whooping or cursing you out. You grow up with this "love" and this is what you think love is. You can't know what love is if you never had it. Look up the definition. To me God is love and can't anybody love me better than him.

A few more things us ladies need to think about that we say often. "I know my worth," but do you really? Think about that and ask yourself what are you worth?

Do you get that I don't care attitude sometimes and put your worth to the side.

Do you rely on that slogan "money over everything" or are you the type that no matter what he may do you find yourself saying "But, he needs me. I make him better"?

I have a few things for the men to think about. I'm sure men get a raw deal from some ladies because I do believe there are a lot of ladies who will use men, play mind games and give them false hopes on love and relationships. Some men really do love us ladies and still get treated bad and sometimes the men are fools in love also. They with a girl and they deep in love and that same girl is screwing Tom, Dick and Harry. As a matter of fact, Harry could be your best friend and you don't even know it. BE CAREFUL. I see you men who take care of your homes and your kids and you still aren't happy because your girl/wife won't satisfy you sexually nor will she cook dinner. I don't see how you all do it, but I guess that's one reason why you may cheat, huh? I say leave if you aren't happy and find it elsewhere but like I said earlier. "EASIER SAID THAN DONE".

As we close out the year with our December Issue I still say:

DON'T SETTLE. Go into the new year happy and knowing your worth.

Samantha, CEO

CHAPTER 8

NOT TRUE

1:15pm

Samantha decided to call Reggie. As her phone dials his number, she absent-mindedly extends and retracts her writing pen waiting for him to answer.

"Hello, Reggie. How are you?" she said sounding pleasant, in control.

"Hey," Reggie replied sounding genuinely surprised. "I was not expecting a call from you at all."

"I know," she paused, "but I wanted to call and apologize for last night in the bar."

"I was happy to see you. Then you left me on that dance floor by myself. But, it's cool. Besides, you already apologized."

"What are you talking about? I did not. I—" she tried to finish, but Reggie's laughter cut her short.

"Oh, yes, you did."

"I haven't seen you in years. I was so drunk! If I apologized I don't remember." She continued working the pen as she spoke.

"Yeah, ok. Where are you?"

"I'm at the office. I'll be leaving soon."

"Samantha, last night you told me you were married. You said you were sorry for when I called you and that your husband was sitting next to you. Remember? I said, "You got married on me? You were supposed

47

to be *my* wife". Reggie said this all with a slight smile in his voice. She could hear it. *She could damn near see his face with that smile.*

Samantha was looking at her phone and thinking to herself *what is this man talking about?* Her pen she had been working in her hand slowed down a bit, but she barely noticed.

"Reggie, are you smoking or are you high?"

"I don't get high. Are you high?" He laughed out loud at her question. "You told me you have a stepson and a daughter. I congratulated you and your family. You gave another man everything I wanted with you." Although he she still heard him smiling, he seemed a bit serious, too.

"Oh, please. You were with who you wanted to be with and you had your chance with me sooooo long ago."

"Sounds all too familiar," Reggie replied. "Do I need to remind you again about last night?'

"What about last night? You are confusing me. You're just not making sense."

"Oh, damn! Samantha you must have been stoned for real. You have memory loss."

"Huh?"

Samantha drew a complete blank. She tried to recall some of last night. Any of last night. She wasn't getting anything. She was completely clueless so she ran it down:

Went to JClub.
Met Nita and Tee.
Had some drinks.
Danced.
Had some more drinks.
Danced some more.
Had some more drinks.
Saw Reggie.
Ditched Reggie.
Left JClub and went back to hotel.
Called Edward.
Woke up this morning.

"What?" Reggie brought her back to the present and their phone conversation. "I'm about to come to your office really fast to see you before you leave."

"Oh no," her pen faltered in her hand. "You can't come to my office right now. I'll be leaving out real soon." Samantha emphasized the real soon part of her statement.

"I'm on my way," was the last thing he said before ending the call.

That stopped Samantha and her pen work completely. She did not want to see Reggie. Well, she *did,* but that was why she *didn't.* All she could think about was the smell of his cologne from the night before. She thinks *Reggie is crazy* saying things that could not have possibly happened. She hadn't even spoke to him other than on the floor at JClub. Still…how could he know so much about her life now? Besides that she didn't really want to see him. Okay, well she *did,* but, again, that is the same reason why she didn't want to see him. She *couldn't see him.* Shit! She called Nita.

"Niiiitaaaa. Where are you?" she said desperately into the phone when her friend picked up.

"Ummm...home? Why?"

"Reggie about to come to the office," Samantha resumed working her writing stylus, again.

"Really? Your ass called me at 4o'clock this morning telling me he was coming to the hotel. Did he come?"

"Whaaaaaa—? The hotel? Oh shiiit," Samantha dropped the pen from her hand. This was not good. This was soooo not a good thing.

"You forgot?" Nita pressed her.

"Forgot? How can I forget what I don't remember? I don't remember calling you. I don't remember talking to him last night. I remember calling Edward and going to sleep!"

"I told you," Nita said in a voice that dripped of reprimand and a little curiosity, "I told you to take your ass to bed after you hung up with me but you kept saying *but Reggie wants to talk to me."* Nita mocked her playfully whining a bit and slurring her words.

Samantha didn't even register it enough to be upset with Nita. She clearly doesn't remember any of the things that she said let alone talking to Reggie.

"I have to retract. I plead the fifth, and any other amendment I can plead. I swear I can't drink anymore.

"That's a fact, girl. You really can't handle your liquor like you used too. I'm surprised you didn't sleep past check-out time today. Anyway, I'll be there to pick you up around 3:30pm. In the meantime, don't fuck Reggie in your office."

"That's not funny," Samantha replied as her friend laughed.

They hung up

15 minutes later Reggie arrived and Suzanne enters Samantha's office to announce him.

"Mrs. Jones, you have a visitor," she says.

Samantha looks up from her work,

"Send him in. Thanks, Sue."

Suzanne leaves the office and Reggie walks in. He has on an understated designer label blue button up shirt, crisp jeans, is freshly groomed and holding a beautiful bouquet of flowers out to her.

"Samantha, nice to see you again and these flowers are for you," he said in a voice that was smooth as butter.

"Thank you," she said as she stood to take the flowers from him, "how sweet of you."

As she reached for the flowers, Reggie hugged her and snuck a kiss in on her cheek. Samantha pulled away quickly—not because of the kiss but because she found herself intoxicated by his cologne. It was same cologne from the night before.

"You smell uh…," she began and caught herself, "I mean. These flowers smell good."

"It's ok," he laughed, "You smell good, too. Can I get one more hug?"

"No, I can't Reggie. You never change, do you? You will try until I give in," with that, she walked across the office space.

"It worked last night."

This Samantha ignored and acted as if she didn't hear him because all she could think about is what happened in the club.

Reggie walks towards Samantha and grabs her and presses her up against her desk. He starts to lift her skirt up.

"Reggie, what are you doing? She asked"

"What does it look like I'm doing?"

"Right here, right now"

"Why not, it's the perfect place"

"I'm not sure of that Reggie, this is my place of business and one of my workers may need me"

"They will have to wait"

"This is not a good idea"

"I don't live off of good ideas Samantha, you know that. I'm the bad guy and the opportunity is now so just relax, clothes your eyes and live in this moment"

Samantha couldn't resist his touch or his smell. Something about him made her close her eyes and act as if she didn't care about anything at that moment. As her eyes were closed her breathing got heavy.

"You missed this, didn't you? I bet you remember this", Reggie asked.

Reggie continued to rub on her uncontrollably while tasting her goods. He took one of her legs and raised it on his shoulder as he continued to lick in between her legs. He took his fingers and played with her as he licked her at the same time. Samantha tried her best to remain as silent as possible so her workers didn't get any suspicions. Reggie slowly made his way up unbuttoning her shirt and begins to caress her breast as he took his mouth and carefully took his time licking and sucking on her nipples. Samantha released a moan and she told him not to stop. Reggie took that as his chance to go all the way. He unbuttoned his pants, pulled them down and sat in Samantha's chair. He ordered her to come to him and sit on his dick. Samantha did not refuse; she lifted her skirt up and sat backwards on him. They engaged in this act for about 3 minutes and Samantha realized what she was doing was wrong. She jumped up and fixed her clothes.

"Reggie, I can't do this"

"You already did it", he said

"I can't continue it"

"You liked it, didn't you? Be honest"

"Yes, you know we never had a problem in that area"

"I missed you Samantha, you were always my down chick and we had good times together"

"Reggie, you know nothing can come from this, it's been years and I've moved on" "I know you have your life and that doesn't include me but I just want to be able to see you more"

"I'm married, what just happened is exactly what it is, it just happened and nothing can come from it"

"Do you love your husband", he asked.

"I sure do Reggie"

"I still love you, I think this was meant to happened between us"

"I don't think it was meant, it just happened. I got lost in the moment"

"I guess that's what you will say about last night too, did that just happened Samantha"?

"I don't know what you talking about Reggie"

"Samantha, why did it work last night? Why did you give in?"

"What did I give into Reggie?"

"You let me hold you. You let me kiss on you. We had a long talk."

"You know, Reggie, I don't remember anything from last night."

"You're lying," he said shortening the distance between them. "You called me and said *come visit me in the hotel, I can't sleep* and I came."

Oh shit! she thought. It was all coming back to her. She did say that but not to Reggie.

"I remember saying that to my husband about not being able to sleep," she said then spun around, "Fuck! Are you serious Reggie? Did you take advantage of me?"

"Never would I do that, Samantha. You wanted me too. You were all over me and I pushed you away because you kept saying *I can't. I'm married but I want to.*"

"This is a nightmare," she sighed as she ran her fingers through her hair and pulled it at the scalp as if she was trying to jolt herself out of sleep. As if that sensation would override the sinking feeling in her stomach. "I'm sorry Reggie. That was not me last night, and I swear it was somebody else. We didn't do anything did we?"

"No, I did a lot to you but you didn't do anything back," he said. That reassured her until he added, "You still taste the same, and I love tasting you"

"That doesn't sound too good."

The more Samantha thought about the night before, the more she began to recall. What she thought was a dream had really happened.

"I thought you were in my dream, like seriously. It was real? I remember what I thought was a dream and if that occurred, that's some bullshit and that means I cheated on my husband, not once but twice. I never would have did this today if I would have knew or remembered last night"

She paced the floor, still holding her head as she walked back and forth.

"Samantha, calm down. I'm joking. It's cool. Nothing happened. We didn't do anything. I knew you were drunk. We had great conversation and I know you love your husband. As much as I wanted to have you, I knew it wasn't mutual but today it was. I mean, the man you wanted was your husband last night but I was the one you needed today. It just wouldn't have been right last night. We just laid there and I held you until you fell asleep. I didn't take off your clothes or anything. You woke up in your clothes, right? You still sexy as hell! I wanted you bad as hell last night but you were scared. I had to respect that."

Reggie moved in towards Samantha closing the distance completely this time. He grabbed her by her waist taking his hands and rubbing through her hair and rested his finger tips on the back of her neck. He whispered in her ear "I will always love you". For a brief moment, Samantha had felt something. His cologne and his whisper had gotten her bothered again. Reggie pulled her closer, turned her around and sat her on the desk and kissed her. Samantha pulled back immediately.

"Reggie, I think you should go. You shouldn't be here."

"So, when you call me I come and now you kick me out of your office."

"Reggie, promise me that you won't say anything about seeing me or last night or what happened in this office."

"I can't make a promise," he shrugged.

"What the fuck you mean?"

"When you called I was out with a friend. I told them I had to leave to check on you."

"What friend? *Did you say my name?*"

"I said *a friend who is visiting.* I may have said your name, but I don't think so."

"Great! Just fucking great, Reggie," Samantha rolled her eyes at him adding sarcastically, "Thanks a lot."

"Nobody knows who I was talking about."

"Yeah, right. I hope not. You can leave now," Samantha said dismissing him.

"Whaaa—?? Damn! It's like *that*?" Reggie stared at her in disbelief.

"Hell yes! It's *exactly like that*," she all but spat emphasizing the last three words. "It's my fault for even calling you last night. Please don't call me anymore and take this information to the grave with you. My husband will kill us both."

Reggie laughed a gut-busting laugh as if that was the funniest thing he had heard all year. When he was able to finally catch his breath he said, "I'd kill him before he'd kill me. You know what Samantha? I wish you a happy life. I will leave you alone and don't you ever get drunk and call me." With that, he stormed out of her office snatching the door open, but not slamming it.

He was upset. Oh, he was mad. Samantha, however, was in disbelief, scared, shocked and at a loss for words. She ended up telling the only friend she could trust which was Nita.

(Phone Conversation)

"Nita"
"Hey, whats up"
"I did it, I feel awful. Like I'm about to cry"
"What did you do"?
"I became her"
"Girl, what you talking about. Who did you become"?
"The office Slut, The cheating wife.....a Hoe"
"You crazy, so you fucked Reggie in the office"?
"Only for a few minutes but he gave me head too"
"Was it at least good"?
"Yes, but that's not the point. I had no condom. I made a horrible mistake"
"I can't believe you. In your office? You better hope Edward never finds out or you're dead"
"I know, I don't think Reggie will say anything"
"Girl please. He not keeping that to himself. You know how men talk".
"I told him I can't see him anymore and I told him not to contact me"
"I'm sure he didn't listen to that. Reggie is crazy"
"I know. He left out of here mad. Why can't he just be happy with what he got and leave me alone"

"He's a man. He had a piece of you and you suppose to belong to another man. The fact that you even went there with him makes him feel like he already won and it also may make him feel like you used him"

"I wish I would have never engaged in anything with him and I can't even blame this on alcohol"

"Send me your will because if Edward ever finds out you know he will go crazy"

"I can't stomach this. I think I'm going to be sick. I have to go take a hoe bath in my office bathroom before I catch this flight home"

"You still a slut" (she laughs)

"Thanks a lot Nita, way to rub it in. It was a mistake"

"Get yourself together, don't stress about it. I'll see you in a few to take you to the airport"

Samantha let moments of feeling lonely with the mixture of being drunk give Reggie something to talk about. Not only that, but made him feel like she still wanted him when he came to the office. The trip that was the best thing that happened also turned into the worst thing that happened.

CHAPTER 9

I'M SORRY

Samantha was home, again, and she hadn't heard from Reggie since she left Atlanta over a week ago. She thought about changing her phone number but she had too many important connects. She could have just as easily blocked his number. For some reason, she didn't even do that. She just put it behind her and went on with life. She did ask God to forgive her one night while praying and she made a promise never to cheat with another man again. Samantha and Edward had movie night 2 days before Christmas and they went out afterwards for a few drinks. Samantha enjoys going out with her husband because they rarely get to enjoy each other's time due to their work schedules. Samantha always feels the love gets stronger when they have alone time together.

Luke 12:3

"Whatever you have said in the dark will be heard in the light and what you have whispered behind closed doors will be shouted from the housetops for all to hear"

Christmas Eve

Edward came home from work three hours early. Samantha was cleaning up the kitchen and listening to Christmas songs. Things between them had been great and they were prepared for Christmas to exchange gifts, do the family dinner and enjoy the holiday season.

Edward announced his arrival by walking in and slamming the door.

"Who the fuck is Reggie, Samantha?" he asked loudly and with a dead serious face.

Caught completely by surprise, Samantha had a confused look on her face.

"Edward, what are you talking about?"

"You'd better answer me Sam. I'm not going to ask you but one last time. Who the fuck is Reggie?" Edward spoke this time quietly and deliberately.

Jr. heard his father so he came downstairs running into the kitchen.

"Dad, I need to show you something."

"Jr., go to your room," Edward said not taking his eyes off Samantha.

"But Dad, it's—," Jr. tried to continue but was cut short.

"I said go to your room. NOW."

With that, Jr. looked at his father wide-eyed, slowly backed out of the kitchen and went to his room.

"Baby," Samantha began, "I need you to calm down and we can talk. Reggie is nobody."

"*Nobody*, huh? Apparently he is *somebody*. Somebody you *fucked*! You fucking ex-boyfriends now, Samantha?" Edward asked, the veins in his neck standing out.

"He is an ex," Samantha said refusing to back down, "and no, I'm not fucking ex-boyfriends."

"Don't play with me Sam. I will fuck you up. Don't you lie. Did you fuck him or not?"

"No," She answered coolly. "Where did you get that wrong information from?

"Do you know how many niggas I know in Atlanta? Do you?" Edward said hotly. "I used to be in the streets, remember? How I hear *Samantha- that-magazine-owner was with Reggie*? How I hear that shit if you wasn't with him?"

"That's a lie. I didn't sleep with him, Edward."

"Did you *see him*?"

"He was at the club the night me and my girls went out."

Edward grabbed Samantha and pulled her arm real tight. Maintaining his hold, he pulled her in the bathroom downstairs and slammed the door behind them.

"Bitch, don't lie to me," Edward said as he pushed her against the wall.

Samantha was shocked at first. Then she was scared as hell. She had never seen this side of Edward and she didn't know what to say or do but she knew she couldn't admit to anything besides seeing him in the bar.

"Edward," she finally broke down. With a shaky voice and tears flowing she continued, "I promise you, baby, I didn't sleep with that man. Don't call me a bitch."

"You will be a sorry bitch if you married to me and fucking other niggas."

"If I said *yes I did*, would you be happy? I'm telling you *no, I didn't* and you don't believe me."

"If you say *yes*, you will be on this bathroom floor begging for your life. Hell, you will wonder if you will get to breathe your next *breath*! Tell me the truth because if I ask in the streets back at home, I will find out."

"I seen him at the club," Samantha began, "I walked away and left him on the dance floor. He left. He showed up at my office the next morning and brought me flowers and tried to kiss me. That's the truth I swear. I kicked him out the office."

"So you kissed him and you accepted the flowers?"

"I didn't kiss him. He tried to kiss me. The flowers meant nothing. Baby I swear"

Samantha couldn't finish her sentence before Edward slapped her face. Samantha stood there for a few seconds before she ran out the bathroom, upstairs to their room, and slammed the door. She was *so* scared. She just wanted him to believe her.

She heard Edward as he came up the stairs. She hadn't locked the door, so all he had to do was open it and he was walking towards her. She grabbed the clock off the night stand and threw it at him. Samantha fought through heavy sobs that wracked her body.

"You...you...you fucking bastard!" chest heaving she shouted, "I will fuck you up if you ever put your hands on me again!"

"How was the kiss, huh? I do everything for you and you go to Atlanta and get up with an ex?" Edward laughed bitterly. "Ain't this some shit? Do I mean anything to you? You let him in your office? I can't believe shit you say right now," he spat.

"I didn't do anything, Edward! I pulled away from him. He tried. I promise you! Please believe me. I would never cheat on you. I love you. I wouldn't do that to you babe. They are lying, he lying."

"So, I need to go to Atlanta and find him and fuck him up for lying on you? Do you care if I fuck him up?"

"No, He is nobody Edward. It's not worth it."

They were interrupted by a knock at the door. It was Jr..

"Let me in. What's going on in there?"

"It's okay, Jr. We just talking," Samantha said trying to sound less scared and frantic than she actually was. The little boy wasn't fooled.

"No it's not ok, let me in."

Samantha looked at Edward. His anger was a strong and fresh as when he walked in the house. Sitting on the side of the bed, holding his head, he whispered to Samantha.

"I will fuck you up, know that. Don't make me."

Edward trailed off as he got up to open the door. As soon as he did, Jr. ran to Samantha.

"I'm fine, Jr.," she said folding him in her arms"

"You're crying though," he said with disbelief.

"Yeah. Your dad and I are not agreeing on some things right now."

"Jr., you can go back you your room," Edward tried to convince him everything was ok. "It's cool. You have my word."

"Okay," the boy agreed, but you could tell he didn't belief his dad.

"I love you son," Edward added.

Without another word or a second look, Jr. left out the room and Edward closed the door behind him. Once he thought Jr. was out of earshot, he turned to Samantha and whisper-shouted through clenched teeth and a tight jaw.

"Sam, you made me do this shit! Clean this shit up in this room! You and these Atlanta trips gone have to stop!"

"My business is there," Samantha protested.

"Do you *think* I *care* about that? I can't trust it. Your husband and your family are here, Samantha, in Tampa!

"You don't trust me, so don't be with me."

"Sam, just shut up ok? *Just shut up.*"

"Wait, naw. You believe the streets over your wife? How you think I feel?"

"I hear shit about my wife, what you think I feel? That damn near killed me. I couldn't work after that just thinking about that shit in my head. I wanted to smash your head as soon as I came in the door."

"You hit me Edward. *You fucking hit me.* Like really, my husband hit me. You need to leave. You can't stay here tonight."

"Leave? My house? You are tripping. Aint nobody leaving."

"GET OUT! JUST GO!" Samantha screamed at the top of her lungs.

Falling across the bed, she curled into an impossibly tight ball and started to cry. Edward left out the room. An hour had passed and

Samantha got up to see if Edward was downstairs, but he was gone. Jr. was in his room still up.

"Jr.," Samantha asked while peeking her head in the boy's room, "did your dad leave?"

"Yes," he answered, "he said he would be back. He went to the store."

Samantha went back to the room and called Edward's cell phone at least five times but no answer. She decided to go back to sleep. She figured he was mad and probably needed his space. She never thought they would ever get to this point. She thought about calling her mom but then she changed her mind because she knew her mom would just tell her to leave him or come to Atlanta for a few days. Samantha was happy Aniya wasn't home but she also thought if she was there maybe Edward would not have took it that far.

4:11am
The phone rings. Samantha answers half sleep.
"Hello?"
"Mrs. Jones?" a voice on the other end asks.
"Yes, this is Mrs. Jones."
"Mrs. Jones, this is Dr. Hall from Tampa Emergency Hospital.
We need you to get here if you can. We have Edward Jones here in the Emergency room."
"Now? He is there? Now? What happened? What's wrong?"

Samantha frantically fired off one question after another not even bothering to wait for the doctor's response to the one before. She hung up the phone and called Edward's mom to tell her to come to the house with Jr. Although he was old enough to stay by himself, she didn't know when she'd be back home.

CHAPTER 10

LORD, I NEED YOU

8:56am Christmas Morning

"Lord, I need you now. Lord, need you now," Samantha sang. "Lord right now."

She started to pray.

"Lord, I'm sorry for all my sins and not acknowledging you for all my blessings. I need you now like I've never needed you before. Please save my husband, he doesn't deserve this. He is a good man. I can't live without him. Please help God."

As she closed her prayer, she found she couldn't stop crying. She touched Edwards hand and kissed his forehead. He was banged up pretty bad, non-responsive and in intensive care heavily medicated. It was at this time Dr. Hall came to her side.

"Mrs. Jones, your husband is under a lot of medication and we have to keep him that way. He is lucky to be alive still. He was driving at least 100mph and lost control of his truck slamming into a pole. The truck is totaled.

"Jesus, help me," Samantha's voice caught in her throat as her hand flew to her chest. "Doctor… was he drinking?"

"No, no alcohol involved."

"Thank God," she said breathlessly. Then she continued, "He's not a drinker, but after last night I thought maybe he decided to start."

"We are sorry," was the doctor's reply.

"It's too early to tell. I'm sorry. I'll leave you with your husband."

The doctor walks out leaving Samantha alone with her husband and her thoughts. She began to speak to him.

"Edward, can you hear me? I need you to live. We need you. The kids need you. You have to fight. You better not leave me."

Samantha sat there with Edward all morning, not taking her eyes off of him. Edward's mom eventually came to the hospital with Jr. Edward was still in the ICU. Jr. couldn't see his dad, but Edward's mom could. Samantha decided to take Jr. to the cafeteria.

"Samantha, is my dad going to be ok?" he asked with a look of worry and concern beyond that of most little boys.

"I believe God will make it all better."

"Can I tell you a secret? And promise not to tell my dad."

"I promise."

"My dad use to fight my Mom real bad and he would always send us to our room."

"Oh honey, I and your dad never fight. This was just a bad situation but it won't happen again."

"My dad gets crazy sometimes. It's scary."

"You don't worry about that Jr. You just worry about him fighting for his life. Do you know how to pray?"

"A little bit."

"I need you to pray for your dad a lot."

Samantha hugged Jr. while holding back tears because she didn't know if he would make it or not. The thought of Jr. losing his dad killed her inside.

Samantha's phone rang.

"Merry Christmas, Mommy."

"Hey Baby Cakes," she replied to Aniya. "You beat me to the call. Did Santa bring you lots of gifts?"

"Yes, dolls, and princess stuff."

"That's wonderful, I'm happy for you."

"Mommy can I speak to Edward and Jr.?"

"You can speak to Jr. He is right here. Hold on baby.

Samantha handed Jr. the phone and told him not to tell Aniya any sad news.

Hours had passed and they were at the hospital all day and night. Jr went home with his grandmother while Samantha stayed at the hospital. It was about 8:30pm and Samantha just sat there looking at Edward. She started singing a gospel song. "Alone in a room, it's just me and you. I feel so lost cause I don't know what to do". That was one of her favorite gospel songs by Yolanda Adams. She continued to sing and she started crying. Samantha closed her eyes and just rested her head as close to Edwards shoulder as she could get. She whispered

Through the good and the bad, sickness and in health, till Dea…

She paused. She couldn't finish it with the word death and the thought of it made her sick to her stomach all over again. She heard a moan and looked up to see Edward struggling to move and open his eyes. Grabbing his hand, she felt him move and try to hold hers firmly. She immediately pressed the call button for the nurse. "Edward, I'm here baby. I'm here baby," she whispered to him, raising her head toward Heaven she added, "Thank you God.

The nurses rushed in and asked her to leave out. Samantha didn't want to, but she knew she had to, but before she left out she saw a tear drop from Edward's eye.

While waiting outside the room, the doctor came and told her that Mr. Jones was doing much better. "He will be fine. It's a miracle he survived with only bumps and bruises. No internal injuries at all," the doctor said. He had never seen anything like it. Samantha dropped to her knees after hugging that doctor.

"Thank you, Lord, for your miracle. Thank you Father," she rejoiced
"We have to keep him a few days for observation. As soon as one becomes available we will move him to his own room."

Samantha was so relieved. They moved him the next morning to a room.

"Samantha, I love you baby. I'm sorry. I'm so sorry for hurting you," Edward said looking truly sorry.
"Hey, stop that. We need you out of here. We will get through this. I love you too," she said as she stroked his palm with her fingertips.
"I was mad. I was so angry…. I was speeding… and…" his voice trailed off and she gently placed a finger to his lips.
"Edward hush. Just hush. It's ok. All that matters is you are still here and I prayed so hard even Jr prayed. We got our prayers answered and this will be a Christmas I will never forget. I believe in miracles. God is so good…"

Now it was Samantha who trailed off as she hung her head and the tears began to fall from her eyes. Edward exhaled loudly as he took her chin in his hand, lifting her to meet his gaze.

"Aww, hell. Don't start that crying shit," his voice softening in contrast. "You know I hate when you cry."
"Yup. Edward is back. I know you do. My Poopsie is back."
"I'm ready to go home so I can make love to you or have rough make up sex."
"Only you would think like that laid up in a hospital bed."
"My dick still work, watch…just jump on it," Edward said as he tried to rise up and reach for her.

"I will not, Edward," Samantha said playfully, but firmly pushed him back down on the bed. "The doctor said you can't have sex for 2 months."

"Bullshit!" Edward shouted in a whisper.

They both laughed. Edward was released a week after the accident so needless to say they spent Christmas in the hospital.

New Year's Eve

"Baby, hurry up and get ready."

Edward was already dressed and, as usual, Samantha still wasn't even close to being dressed.

"I'm trying to decide what to wear," Samantha was putting lotion on her smooth brown skin starting with her long legs.

"I'm sure whatever you put on will be ok, you have a million and one dresses in that closet. Just pick one," Edward said sitting on the bed.

"Do you like my hair?"

"What is that style called?"

"It's an up-do."

"It's definitely UP, but it's nice. I like your curly hair better."

"You don't like it. I knew you wouldnt.

"For tonight it's nice. You know it will be messed up after we get home."

"No its not," Samantha laughed "No sex for you buddy."

"I'm not listening to what you say. That up-do is coming down."

Samantha pulls out a silver and black dress and holds it up to her body while looking in the mirror.

"Ok, what about this one?"

"That's nice, just hurry up. I'm almost ready. If you wear that, I'll put on my silver and red tie."

"Okay. I just need to find the right shoes…."

Sighing heavily, Edward turns to Samantha, "We will be staying right here in this house if you don't hurry up *and* you still have to do your make-up.

"No-Poopsie, the make-up is all natural today so it won't take long."

Thirty minutes later Samantha was finally ready. Edward was sitting in the living room trying not to get upset waiting for his slow wife. As Samantha walked in he eyed her from head to toe.

"Damn, baby. You trying to give me a heart attack? You
are so beautiful and that dress is bangin' on you."

"Thanks honey." Holding a pair of shoes in her hand, she reached down to slip them on. "I guess I'll wear these red heels tonight." Across the room, Edward acted as if he is about to faint. "Red pumps make a brother weak," he said as he stood up and walked towards Samantha and grabbed her by her waist. He began slow dancing with her right in the living room.

"So we dancing with no music tonight?"

"Just live in this moment. in my head I'm hearing Slow Jam by R.Kelly," holding her closer he whispers, "I love you Sam. Everything about you."

"I love you too," she whispers back before pulling her head back to look in his eyes and kiss him softly on the cheek.

"Now wipe that lipstick off my cheek."

"Nope. It has to stay on. It's a tattoo for the night right on your face."

"So I know it's real, right?" he laughs. "I'm so happy my Mom gave us these tickets to this New Year's Ball."

"Me, too. We need this. We haven't been out together in so long. The night will be beautiful."

While walking to the event Edward wanted to take a picture of Samantha before they went inside. He told her to stand by this brick wall with her hands around her waist and look the opposite way. Samantha thought it was silly but she did what he asked her to do.

"I think we have a winner for the night," Edward shouted loud enough to turn a few heads.

"Edward, you so crazy but that's why I love you. You compliment my sexy tho' because that tie is everything," she said cocking her head to the side a little bit. "You don't look so bad yourself in that suit."

"Let's just go inside and dance the night away. I just want to hold you in my arms all night."

"You got me for the rest of your life.

Against all odds

Samantha and Edward fought to keep their marriage together and they promised each other no matter what they would make it work. They started going to church as a family after Edward's accident and they took time out and had date nights twice a month.

Samantha's magazine was number #1 in the south and she kept her office in Atlanta but also opened one in Tampa, she let Suzanne do the majority of the work at the Atlanta office.

Edward loved Samantha unconditionally and made a promise to never hit her again.

To both of their surprise a year later Samantha was pregnant. She wasn't happy about it because, with the success of the magazine, she didn't have time for a baby but she was happy that it was with her husband and not anyone else's. After all she had gone through, she finally had happiness. She learned how to let someone love her, be submissive to their love and trust them with her happiness.

Message:

In any relationship, friendship or marriage it takes work. It's not an easy task. It takes a lot of give and take as well as compromising. Anything worth fighting for is worth keeping. Everyday will not be easy but if two people are willing to put forth the effort to make it work it definitely can be done. "Don't give up on what never gave up on you".

Samantha, as we know, is very successful when it comes to handling her business. She has a beautiful family and a man who truly adores her. With all these great things going on in her life you would think she couldn't make any wrong decisions, right? Samantha almost lost it all with one bad decision that almost cost her everything.

Samantha's problem has always been "being too independent" she is usually giving orders, so it's hard for her to take orders. In "I Became Her" Samantha received papers stating that Aniya's father was going for full custody of their daughter after not being in her life for the first year. Samantha was upset about the entire situation.

Will Samantha lose this battle?

The person sometimes with what we see as "the perfect life" is not always happy inside. Samantha has her career on lock and her beauty is breath taking but something is missing from her life.

"A child with a married man brought a custody battle"
"A women with trust issue's brought doubts"
"Sex brought pleasure"
"A good man brought love"
"Betrayal brought violence"
"Hurt and violence brought pain"
"Pain almost cost someone their life"

Published by Author Latrice Gleen
Book Design by AugustPride

LATRICE GLEEN
AUTHOR

Make Up Artist; Michelle Carter

You create your own insecurities
You have to let someone love you
You have to trust someone with your heart
Not everyone is out to use or abuse you
You have to let go of the past
You have to allow the new to come into your life
You have to seek God for understanding
Not everyone is out to use or abuse you
You have to know your worth
You have to know you should be treated like a queen
You have to act like a queen
Not everyone is out to use and abuse you
You have to know that you are worthy of true love
Somebody is out there for you
Somebody is watching you
Somebody is waiting for you
Somebody wants to love you unconditionally
Not everyone is out to use or abuse you

Author Latrice Gleen

Thank You all for your support

Personal (shout out's) Acknowledgments:

Doris E. Brooks - Love Mom

Jerry Stover

Joyce Adams

Allen Brooks

Thadford Brooks

Jeanette Vaughn

Michelle Brooks

Congratulations to you on your third book. - Wayne, Tamara and Ava

God bless you Tricey, continued success. – K.P.

Good luck and God Bless! – Walt Henigan

Mad love to my sis! Congrats, and I look forward to reading many more of these – Love Bear. Hi Haters

Tanza Green (Taz) Club 77

Melvin Redleman

Sonya Ford

RIP Van Dario McDaniel. My superman, my angel. – Chanel McDaniel

To my very very very very good friend that I met back in 2003. I am so happy for you that you have accomplished part 2 of I Became Her. Congratulations. Love Angie +6

I'm so proud of the women that you have become. Keep up the great work. We love you. – Rian and Rhonda Sat'chell

Congratulations on writing your third book Tricey!!! Wishing you an abundance of success on all your endeavors. – Your Sister Nette

Tysha Martin, Ramier and Raleigh – We love you

Love, Gregory and Beverly Crenshaw

Tasha Nicole

The Harrisons

Richard Keith II – Carry Out Café

Congratulations sis on your third book. I'm very happy for you and proud of your accomplishments. Always keep God first in your life, listen to your heart, continue to pursue your dreams and you will remain that beautiful person you are inside and out.
Love you! Baby Yo

Business Acknowledgments:

The New Golden Nugget - 2046 Fillmore Ave. Bflo, NY 14214 (716)834-3967

Club 77- Richard & Renee (Owners) - 1614 Broadway St. Bflo, NY (716) 897-2564
The Smaller the club, the bigger the party!

Trice's Tasty Treats! Mon-Sat.10am-6pm (716) 207-6924
Each exquisite bite is a heavenly creation.

Buffalo Raven little league football and cheerleading organization.
Ages 5-13! Come out and have some fun.
Contact **buffaloravensfootball@gmail.com** (716)578-8454

Doris Records (since 1962) CEO Mack Luchey 286 E. Ferry St. Buffalo NY (716)883-2410 Hip Hop, R&B, Blues, Jazz and Gospel
716 Ent

Myracle Catering www.facebook.com/myraclecatering (716) 241-1741

Beyond Cards – Personalized handmade cards for any occasion.
(716)225-3859
Email:beyondcards15@gmail.com
Instagram: BEYONDCARDS
facebook.com/beyond.cards.1

Shop with a brand that stands for Brilliance. **www.iamoyab. bigcartel.com**
Google #OYAB

Author Tanisha D. Mackin Website: **www.tanishadmackin.com**

Shareef Contracting (716) 907-3868

Kool V. Productions

Classic Man Baber Shop – Walter – Professional hair grooming for men and children. 1785 Hertel Ave. Buffalo NY 14216

Total Life Changes **www.iasotea.com/KimmsTea Rep#4028231**

Avion – Hostess/Bartender – Club 77, Indulge & The New Golden Nugget.
"If It Aint About The Money"
Shout out to my Hairdresser Kia Day. Located at 2335 Main – Andre D'Andre's
Open Tues-Sat. Walk INS welcome!

New Style Records - 2995 Bailey Ave, Buffalo NY 14215 (716) 834-0710

Brian Davis – Indulge (Buffalo on Chippewa) and Western New York Imaging Group

Frost Entertainment & JJCD UNLIMITED

Javaughn Harris- Manes Maven Hair Boutique - 5804 Monroe Rd. Charlotte NC 28212 Beauti Bombshells – Charlotte Metropolitan and surrounding areas.

Styles Clothing Design – 1012 Kensington Ave. Buffalo NY 14215 (716) 622-4106 Email:jbrwn8@gmail.com

YOUR SUCCESS, ULTD U Living the Dream!
Deidre D. Brooks, Certified Life Coach (216) 407-2548

NatachaGoreeLLC
Natachagoree.paycation.com- Travel bookings!
"No group is too big or small I can do day trips, weekend getaways cruises" etc_

Natachatags.bigcommerce.com
Coming soon: Hashtag t-shirt line! Be on the lookout. (website Novemeber 1st)
Natasha Intimate Shopping Services – Providing personal shopping services for men that need help shopping for their significant other.

Deep Well Ministries
This ministry promotes gathering people together to seek God. We partner with churches to erase the line that has been drawn between denominations & genders. We partner with organizations to bridge the gap between religion & community organizations.
For more information contact the Founder: Rev. Rachelle Sat'chell Robinson. Email:rev.rsr@deepwellministries.com
Website: www.deepwellministries.com
Twitter-@rev_RSR Instagram: rev_RSR
Facebook.com/deepwellministries

FROM THE AUTHOR

Thank you all for your continuous support. I appreciate all the love. I have to give a personal thank you to God for allowing me to continue on this journey. Without him there would be no me or the gift that he gave to me. I'm blessed even when I can't see it.

Thank you to Tommi for her support and allowing me to use her on the cover of my book once again. She is a beautiful person inside and out and I truly mean that. #myBGR

Thank you to my Publishing Company "Authorhouse" who I've worked with since 2011. They have helped make my dreams come true.

Thank you to Stacey Bowers for taking the time out to help design this BANGIN book cover.

I have to extend big hugs and kisses to my babies. All my nieces, nephews and God daughters. TT loves you all. #mytrueinspirations

I wish everyone PEACE in their mind and LOVE in their hearts. Life is too short and your entire life can change in one blink of an eye. Forgive and move on.

Tricey 2015

ABOUT THE AUTHOR

Latrice Gleen is an amazing author who makes all her stories come to life. Born and raised in Buffalo, New York, she never let where she's from stop her from where she's going. Latrice started writing and publishing books in 2010. Latrice believes everyone has a story and everyone can relate to each story she writes. Latrice has been through life's journey, and in some of her life situations, she's also "became her" and can relate to the characters inside her books. Latrice wishes that everyone takes all the positives out of her books and learn something from them, which will help change their lives.

"If you remain positive, the negative things and people will eventually die off because they won't have anything to feed off of to give them life" -Author Latrice Gleen

Printed in the United States
By Bookmasters